Because the story is so easily remembered, children will be able to retell it quite quickly, using some words from the book and some of their own.

The little pig said, "No, no, I won't let you in."

What's "fortune"?

It means the mummy pig sent them off to earn some money.

Talking together about the story, the words and the pictures gives children the chance to tell you about the book and ask questions. This helps them to find out more about the story and shows you what they understand.

# For Felicity

First published 2001 by Walker Books Ltd
87 Vauxhall Walk
London SE11 5HJ

This edition published 2007

10 9 8 7 6 5 4 3 2 1

Illustrations © 2001 Rachel Merriman
Introductory and concluding notes © 2001
CLPE/LB Southwark

This book has been typeset in
Stempel Schneidler

Printed in China

British Library Cataloguing in Publication Data:
a catalogue record for this book
is available from the British Library

ISBN 978-1-4063-1412-0

www.walkerbooks.co.uk

# Reading Together
# The Three Little Pigs

To Harvey
love
Santa
x

# Read it together

The traditional tale of *The Three Little Pigs* is a favourite with many children. What's special about these little pigs is that they live in the city.

> I like it when the wolf huffs and puffs.

Children enjoy having traditional tales like this read to them again and again. It helps them to build up a rich store of known stories and makes sharing books even more enjoyable.

The repetition and the pattern of three in the story help children to guess what happens next and to join in. This builds their confidence in reading.

> And then...

> The naughty wolf blew the house down and gobbled up the little pig.

# The Three Little Pigs

Illustrated by **Rachel Merriman**

WALKER BOOKS

AND SUBSIDIARIES

LONDON · BOSTON · SYDNEY · AUCKLAND

Once upon a time
there was an old mother pig
with three little pigs,
and as she had not enough
to keep them, she sent them out
to seek their fortune.

The first little pig set off, and he met
a man with a bundle of straw.
"Please, Man," said the pig, "give me
that straw to build a house."

The man gave him the straw,
and the first little pig built his house.

Then along came a wolf
and knocked at the door,
and said, "Little pig,
little pig, let me come in."
The little pig answered,
"No, no, by the hair of
my chinny chin chin!"
So the wolf said, "Then I'll huff
and I'll puff and I'll blow your
house in."

And the wolf huffed and he puffed
and he blew the house in,
and he ate up the first little pig.

The second little pig
met a man with a
bundle of sticks.

"Please, Man," said the pig, "give me
those sticks to build a house."
The man gave him the sticks,
and the second little pig
built his house.

Then along came the wolf
and knocked at the door,
and said, "Little pig,
little pig, let me come in."
The little pig answered,
"No, no, by the hair of
my chinny chin chin!"
So the wolf said, "Then I'll huff
and I'll puff and I'll blow your
house in."

And the wolf huffed and he puffed,
and he puffed and he huffed,
and at last he blew the house in,
and he ate up the second little pig.

The third little pig met a man
with a load of bricks.
"Please, Man," said the pig,
"give me those bricks to build a house."
The man gave her the bricks, and the
third little pig built her house.

Then along came the wolf
and knocked at the door,
and said, "Little pig,
little pig, let me come in."
The little pig answered,
"No, no, by the hair of
my chinny chin chin!"
So the wolf said, "Then I'll huff
and I'll puff and I'll blow your
house in."

And the wolf huffed and he puffed,
and he puffed and he huffed,
and he huffed and he puffed,
but he could not blow the house in.

Then the wolf was very angry indeed,
and said he would eat up the little pig,
and he would come down the chimney
to get her.
So the little pig put a huge pot
of water on the stove to boil.

Just as the wolf was coming down the chimney,
the little pig took the lid off the pot, and in fell
the wolf.

So the little pig put the lid on again, and boiled
up the wolf until nothing was left of him.

And the third little pig lived happily ever after.

# Read it again

### Act it out
Acting out this memorable story with small toys enables children to get to know it really well and to use some of the words and phrases from the book as they play.

The first little pig said, "Please, Man, give me that straw."

Then the wolf said...

I'LL HUFF AND I'LL PUFF AND I'LL BLOW YOUR HOUSE IN!

### Play the book
Children enjoy taking part in telling a story. Encourage them to join in by saying aloud what the wolf says. They can try to say it in a wolf-like voice.

Little pig, little pig, let me come in.

No, no, by the hair of my chinny chin chin!

### Draw the story
Children could draw their favourite part of the story. You could add speech balloons to show what the wolf and little pig are saying.

## Who'd be a wolf?

Lots of traditional stories have wolves in them.
What are the wolves like in these stories? Are real wolves like that?
Perhaps you could find a fact book and learn about wolves together.

## Rhyme time

Children enjoy playing with language, and rhyming is something they often do by themselves. Huff and puff, bricks and sticks – what other rhyming words can they remember or make up to match words from the story?

## Other versions

There are many other versions of this traditional tale. Look out for them in libraries and bookshops. You can talk together about the differences you and your child notice. Do you have a favourite?